What Gwyneth's biggest fans have to say:

Hi, Gwyneth!
I hope you will go on making hundreds of books!
I just love them!
Syan

Dear Gwyneth,
I think that all your stories are so very, very magical!
Shayla

Dear Gwyneth,
You are the best author ever!!!!!!!
Lucy, aged 9, London

Dear Gwyneth,
I seriously think you should be the children's
laureate! I am really, really, really looking forward to
your new books! Love, your number one fan,
Sidra

To Gwyneth,
I'd rather read your books over and over
than watch television!
Jordan

Gwyneth Rees is half Welsh and half English and grew up in Scotland. She went to Glasgow University and qualified as a doctor in 1990. She is a child and adolescent psychiatrist, but has now stopped practising so that she can write full-time. Gwyneth is the author of *Mermaid Magic*, *Fairy Dust*, *Fairy Treasure*, *Fairy Dreams*, *Cosmo and the Magic Sneeze* and, for older readers, *The Making of May*, *The Mum Hunt*, *The Mum Detective* and *My Mum's from Planet Pluto*. She lives in London with her two cats.

The Mum Hunt won the Younger Novel category of the Red House Children's Book Award 2004.

Visit www.gwynethrees.com

Gwyneth Rees

The Mum Surprise

This book has been specially written
and published for World Book Day 2006.

World Book Day is a worldwide celebration
of books and reading, and was marked in over
30 countries around the globe last year.
For further information please see
www.worldbookday.com

World Book Day in the UK and Ireland is
made possible by generous sponsorship from
National Book Tokens, participating publishers,
authors and booksellers. Booksellers who accept the
£1 World Book Day Token themselves fund the full
cost of redeeming it.

MACMILLAN CHILDREN'S BOOKS

First published 2006 by Macmillan Children's Books
a division of Macmillan Publishers Limited
20 New Wharf Road, London N1 9RR
Basingstoke and Oxford
www.panmacmillan.com

Associated companies throughout the world

ISBN-13: 978-0330-44299-2
ISBN-10: 0-330-44299-6

1 3 5 7 9 8 6 4 2

A CIP catalogue record for this book is available from
the British Library.

Typeset by Intype Libra Ltd
Printed and bound in Great Britain by Mackays of Chatham plc, Kent

For Isabella Duff

'I can't believe your dad's leaving you alone for the whole weekend,' my friend Holly said when I spoke to her on the phone on Friday after school.

'He's not leaving me alone – he's leaving me with Matthew,' I replied. Matthew is my big brother.

'Well, he may as well be leaving you on your own then. You should totally throw a party!'

'Dad's told Matty he'll kill him if he has a party,' I said. I started to stroke my black-and-white kitten, Hercule, who had come into Dad's room where the phone was and jumped up on the bed.

'Matty's going to be seventeen next month, isn't he?' Holly reminded me. 'He should have an early birthday party. That'd be really cool. Then you can invite me too!'

Although Holly is only thirteen – I'm twelve but I'll be thirteen too in a couple of month's time – she's always really fancied my big brother. Matthew, needless to say, has always rated her as almost as much of a pain as he rates me.

'Jake wants him to have a party too,' I told Holly.

Jake has been Matthew's best friend since infant school – just like Holly has been mine.

'Well, why doesn't he then?' Holly asked. 'It's not like he always does exactly what your dad says, is it?'

'No, but this time he really doesn't want to risk upsetting Dad. His birthday's on a Saturday this year and he wants to take Jennifer to Paris for the day.' Jennifer was his girlfriend. 'Dad says he'll pay for it,' I went on, 'as long as Matty looks after the house properly this weekend – which basically means no party.' I could hear Dad calling for me to come downstairs. 'Look, they're about to leave – I'd better go.'

Dad was going away for the weekend with his girlfriend, Lizzie. Lizzie has been Dad's girlfriend for over a year now and I really like her. She'd moved in with us a few weeks ago, just before Christmas. So far we were all getting along really well, and I was hoping that Dad would propose to her soon so I could get to see how it felt to have a mum at last. My own mother died when I was born, so all I've got to remember her by is some photographs. Even Matty doesn't remember her all that well because he was only four when she died.

I put down the phone and went to join Dad and Matthew in the kitchen. Lizzie was outside, putting things in the car while Dad, who already had his coat on, was writing his mobile number and the number of the cottage where they'd be staying on a

2

sticky to put on our fridge. He'd already written out all the other emergency numbers he could think of and left them there for us too. Dad is a police detective, which Lizzie says is the reason he's a bit overprotective sometimes – because he knows about all the bad things that *could* happen to people. He was showing Matthew each emergency number in turn now, until my brother got impatient and snapped, 'Dad, I'm not stupid. I know if the house goes up in flames I need to call the fire brigade.' He looked at me and added, 'And if Esmie goes missing, I'll just phone the police – but not until I've waited a while so I can take advantage of the peace and quiet.'

'Shut up, Matthew!' I gave him a shove.

Dad frowned. 'I hope you two are going to get on with each other while we're gone.' It was the first time he had ever left us overnight in the house on our own and he was obviously worried, even though he wasn't going to be very far away.

'Dad, we *never* get on – you know that!' Matthew joked, but then he saw Dad's face and quickly added, 'But we'll make a special effort this weekend.' And he shoved me back a lot less roughly than normal.

'Are you ready to go, John?' Lizzie asked, coming into the kitchen. Her cheeks were red from being outside and she was holding the suede gloves with the furry lining that Dad had given her for

Christmas. Lizzie is more laid back than Dad about most things – but I guess that might be because she's not really the one in charge of us.

Matty and I went out to the hallway to see them off. It was dark and cold outside and it was starting to rain. Dad grunted, 'It doesn't look great weather for a weekend in the country.' They were only going to be staying a couple of hours' drive away, in a cottage from where they were planning to do some nice country walks, because Lizzie is into that kind of thing. She had bought Dad some walking boots for *his* Christmas present and declared there was nothing she liked better than walking in the country in the winter when it was all crisp and frosty outside.

'If it rains, you can always curl up together on the sofa with a log fire and get all romantic, can't you?' Matty said, grinning like he was making fun of our father now.

Dad glanced at Lizzie and exchanged a smile with her. 'We'll be back on Sunday afternoon and I'll be phoning at regular intervals to check up on the two of you, OK?'

'You don't need to check up on us, Dad,' Matty told him.

Dad just gave a little laugh that told us he thought otherwise.

As their car pulled out of the driveway, the phone started ringing, so Matty went to answer it while I stayed at the door, waving them off. Dad's car had just disappeared round the corner, and I was about to close our front door, when an ambulance turned into the street.

I stopped to watch where it went. It slowed down as it passed our house and then it parked right outside the house next door. Our next-door neighbour is called Mrs Lewis and she lives on her own with her cat. As I watched, the ambulance men got out and went to ring her front doorbell. Mrs Lewis had to be about eighty and we didn't know her very well. She wasn't very friendly and she hardly ever seemed to have any visitors. Her nasty big bruiser of a tomcat was always coming into our garden to pooh, and since we'd got Hercule two months ago and had a cat flap put in for him, Mrs Lewis's cat had started coming into our house to steal Hercule's food. He also liked to pull down any clean washing that was drying on our radiators and sleep on top of it, which really drove Dad mad. Dad had even been round to speak to Mrs Lewis about it once, but she'd just said, 'Dear me . . . I'll have a word with him about that when he comes home . . .' and Dad had come away feeling a bit stupid.

I put on my coat, left the door on the latch and pulled it shut behind me. It's not that I'm nosy or anything, but we do run a Neighbourhood Watch scheme in our street. I walked down our drive and saw that one of the ambulance men was peering through Mrs Lewis's letter box while the other one was looking in through her front window. The one on the porch called out to his colleague, who came back to join him. Then I heard them calling out Mrs Lewis's name and asking if she could manage to get to the door to open it for them.

That's when I remembered that we had a key to Mrs Lewis's house in case of emergencies. Mrs Lewis didn't trust many people, but she trusted Dad because he was a policeman.

Like I said before, it's not that I'm nosy or anything, but I felt quite excited as I stepped over the low fence between our two driveways and asked, 'Is Mrs Lewis all right?'

The ambulance men turned to look at me and one of them said, 'We can see her on the floor in the hallway, but she can't stand up to open the door for us. You don't know who else might have a key, do you?'

I beamed at him. 'Shall I go and fetch it?'

Matthew was off the phone when I got back to the house and I ran up to his bedroom and went in without knocking. Matthew was lying on his bed. 'Matty, guess what?' I said. 'Mrs Lewis has had an accident or something and there's an ambulance here and everything! They need me to take them the key cos they can't get in.'

I expected him to leap up and come with me, but he didn't. He just kept his head turned away from me.

I didn't have time to wonder what was wrong with him because I had to find the key for next door. After all, there was no time to lose. This could be a matter of life and death, for all I knew! I felt even more excited as I grabbed Mrs Lewis's keys from the kitchen drawer where Dad keeps them and took them out to the paramedics who were still speaking to the old lady through the letter box. At least that meant she wasn't unconscious.

'That's the front-door key, I think,' I told them,

separating it from the back-door one, which was also on the key ring.

One of the men slipped the key into the lock, turned it and carefully pushed the door open. Mrs Lewis was lying on the floor at the bottom of the stairs with the telephone beside her – luckily she kept the phone on a low table in the hallway and that must have been how she'd managed to call for help. 'It's my ankle,' she croaked, wincing in pain. She also had a red mark on her forehead where she must have banged it. 'I tripped over Pixie on the stairs . . .' she told us in a weak voice.

'You tripped over a pixie?' The ambulance men were clearly starting to worry that there might be more wrong with her than they'd originally thought.

'Pixie's her cat,' I explained quickly and, as we spoke, Pixie himself came sauntering out of the living room and hissed at all of us. He was a huge black cat with a white circle around one eye and a white left front paw that made him look like he'd just stepped in a saucer of milk. Both his ears were ragged from all the battles he'd been in and he had bad-tempered dark green eyes.

'He's very nervy, poor dear,' Mrs Lewis gasped, flinching as Pixie walked across her to get to the kitchen, digging in his claws en route.

'We need to take you to hospital to get you checked out, love,' one of the men said as he bent down to examine her leg. 'Is there anyone who can come with you – or meet you at the hospital?'

Mrs Lewis shook her head. 'I'm not going into hospital. I can't leave Pixie alone.'

The other ambulance man looked at me. 'Could your family feed the cat if she has to go into hospital for a few days?'

'Oh, yes,' I said quickly. 'Dad's away this weekend, but Matthew and I will come and do it. Matthew's my big brother.'

Ten minutes later I was walking along beside Mrs Lewis as she was taken out to the ambulance in a wheelchair. Suddenly her wrinkled hand shot out and grabbed my wrist, making me jump. 'Don't let Basil get his hands on my treasure,' she whispered to me in a quaky voice.

'*Basil?*' I repeated as she kept hold of my wrist, which was now starting to hurt. 'Who's that?'

She narrowed her eyes and hissed, 'He'll be round here quick as lightning when he hears what's happened!' She let go of my wrist as her chair was lifted into the back of the ambulance.

'She might be a bit confused with the shock of the fall,' one of the paramedics told me, 'but I'm sure she'll be fine. If she knows you're feeding her cat for her, that'll be a big help. You want us to have a word with your brother before we go?'

I shook my head, stuffing my hands in my pockets. 'It's OK. He'll be cool with it.'

9

As I watched them leave, I thought how *uncool* Matthew had seemed when I'd looked in on him earlier.

Back inside our house, I took off my coat and went upstairs to find Matthew still in his room. He was lying on his bed, facing the wall.

'Matty, what's wrong?' I asked, going in and sitting down beside him. When he completely ignored me, I tapped him lightly on the bum. 'Hey, what is it?'

He turned round and shoved me off his bed. 'Get lost, Esmie!'

Normally I'd have gone off straight away in a huff if he'd spoken to me like that, but something about his face stopped me. He looked like he was struggling not to cry. I immediately wished that Dad hadn't gone away, because, even though he and my brother don't get on all that well a lot of the time, whenever Matty's really upset about anything, Dad is always the one he wants to speak to.

'Matty, tell me what's happened. Was it that phone call? Who was it?'

Maybe because I looked so sympathetic for once, he actually told me what was wrong. 'It was Jennifer. She just dumped me!' And he turned back to face the wall again.

'I knew Jennifer would dump him sooner or later,' Holly said when I phoned her up immediately to tell her what had happened. (Holly and I phone each other a lot even though we see each other every day at school. Dad used to be annoyed because of the phone bill, but since he's switched to a package which includes free local calls, he doesn't fuss as much.) 'You could tell she wasn't really into him,' Holly added. In case you haven't guessed, Holly has never liked Jennifer.

'Yeah . . . well . . . the trouble is – he was really into *her*,' I pointed out.

'We'll have to find a way of cheering him up. Shall I ask Mum if I can come round?'

'Holly, I don't think that's going to cheer him up.'

'Hmm . . . Well, why don't you phone Jake and get *him* to come round?'

So that's what I did, and half an hour later Jake arrived at our house with some beers – which he'd never have dared bring with him if Dad had been there. The two of them stayed in Matty's room for ages with the music turned up really loudly, but eventually they came downstairs to raid our freezer for ice cream and to inform me that my brother had decided to throw a party this weekend after all.

'But Matty, Dad said—'

'Dad's not here, is he?' my brother interrupted. He added that since he'd no longer be going to Paris with Jennifer on his birthday in any case, he had nothing to lose. 'Look, we'll clean up on Sunday and

11

Dad won't even know it happened. Jake and I need to start phoning round now to invite people. Jake's got a mate who's eighteen, who can get some booze for us, so that'll be cool.' He opened the kitchen cupboard and started to pull out bags of crisps. 'I'll get some more of these and people can send out for pizza if they get hungry.'

'Matty, what if—?' But I broke off, because it was a relief to see him back to something like his normal self again and I didn't much feel like arguing with him. A party full of Matthew's mates wasn't going to be a brilliant way to spend Saturday night, but if I got Holly to come over, it might not be too unbearable. Besides, I had something else I needed to ask him. 'Will you come over to Mrs Lewis's with me to feed Pixie? I really don't want to go over there in the dark on my own.' I had already filled him in on what had happened to Mrs Lewis and how I had volunteered to look after Pixie while she was in hospital.

'What a pain!' Matty grumbled.

Swearing under his breath, he led the way round to Mrs Lewis's house, leaving Jake to start phoning people about the party.

We had a job seeing well enough to open the front door when we got there, because there were no lights on. As we stepped inside, the telephone started ringing. Matty and I stood looking at it for a moment, then Matthew picked it up. 'Hello?' He listened for a few seconds, then explained that we were Mrs Lewis's neighbours and that Mrs Lewis had had a fall and been taken into hospital. He listened for a bit longer before saying, 'OK . . . sure . . .' and putting down the phone.

'Who was it?' I asked, keeping a close watch for Pixie, who was known for jumping up on to people's shoulders without warning and digging in his claws as hard as he could to get a better grip.

'Her son – Basil. I didn't even know she had a son, did you?'

'*Basil?*' I stared at him. Until now, I hadn't given any more thought to what Mrs Lewis had whispered to me on her way to the ambulance.

'He says he's going to the hospital tomorrow to visit her,' Matthew continued. 'And then he's coming to the house. He's got his own key, so we won't need to let him in.'

'But Basil's the one she told me to look out for!' I gasped. I quickly told Matthew what Mrs Lewis had said to me about Basil stealing her treasure. 'The ambulance man said she was probably confused – but what if she wasn't? What if Basil's coming here tomorrow to steal something?'

Matthew looked at me warily. 'Esmie, don't start, OK?' (I've got a bit of a reputation for liking to investigate things, you see.)

'I'm not starting!'

'Yes, you are. And you know what Dad said about

how you shouldn't interfere so much in other people's business.'

'He only meant his and Lizzie's business,' I protested. (I had tried to help Dad and Lizzie's relationship along at various points since they'd met – which they hadn't always appreciated.)

'Esmie, just keep your nose out of this, OK?' he snapped.

I glared at him. 'Just chill, why don't you? You're beginning to sound like Dad!'

But, needless to say, as we headed for the kitchen to feed Pixie, I was feeling anything but chilled myself. Instead, I was getting all fired up inside as I kept a sharp lookout for anything that resembled treasure.

❋ 3 ❋

'Maybe the treasure is a really expensive piece of jewellery or something,' Holly suggested when we talked about it on the phone on Saturday morning. It was pouring with rain and Hercule was lying curled up beside me on the sofa, having clearly decided he was spending the day inside.

'I don't know how we can make sure Basil doesn't steal it from her,' I said gloomily. 'He's got a key to her place – so how can we stop him?'

'Maybe Mrs Lewis will get out of hospital today and there won't be time for him to steal anything,' Holly said. She quickly changed the subject back to the one she was most interested in at the moment. 'I'm really glad Matthew's decided to have a party after all. I think Jennifer's really stupid to chuck him, but he's better off without her, he really is. He should totally celebrate!'

'Yeah . . . well . . . he seems pretty miserable again this morning,' I told her. 'I looked in on him earlier but he just yelled at me to get out of his room.'

'Listen, Esmie . . . I've got an idea. Can you hang on for a minute?' Holly left the phone for several minutes and came back sounding excited. 'You know how we said this party could be a sort of early birthday party for Matthew? Well, we should totally make him a birthday cake. I've got Mum's *Celebration Cakes* book here. Listen . . . there's an Aeroplane cake, a Robinson Crusoe Island cake, a Coco the Clown cake . . . those ones are a bit young for Matthew, I reckon . . . oh, but here's one that isn't . . . a Football Match cake. It's basically this big rectangular iced sponge with green desiccated coconut all over it and lines drawn on it in white icing to mark out the pitch. Then you just stick little plastic football players and plastic goalposts on the top. It looks quite easy.'

'I don't know, Holly,' I said warily. 'If we make him a cake it'll have to be pretty cool. Unless . . .' I had just had a thought. I had another idea for a birthday cake. I could hear Matty coming down the stairs, so I told Holly I'd ring her back later.

To my surprise, my brother was fully dressed when he came into the living room. Judging by his pale face and the dark circles under his eyes, I didn't reckon he'd got much sleep the night before. He told me that Jake was coming round this morning and that they were going out together to get some stuff for the party.

'So do people know it's an early birthday party

16

you're having?' I asked. 'Do you think you'll get any presents?'

He snorted. 'It's not that kind of party, you idiot.'

I glanced up at the photograph of our mother that stands on the mantelpiece. In the picture she's got her arms round Matthew and she's also got a big bump sticking out in front of her, which is me. 'That was taken on your *fourth* birthday, wasn't it?' I said.

Matty looked across at the photo too. 'Yep! Now that was the sort of party where you get presents. We had it at home and we played pass the parcel and I remember I wouldn't pass the parcel on when it was my turn. I think Dad had to intervene!'

As I went upstairs to my room, I thought about how I'd never had the sort of birthday party where you played pass the parcel and musical chairs and stuff like that. My parties had nearly always been at Burger King or the ice-skating rink or some other place where Dad could pay for someone else to organize everything.

In my bedroom, I looked at the photograph of my mother that sits by my bed. I'd asked Lizzie if she minded me having it there when she first moved in with us and she'd said that of course she didn't. Just so that she didn't feel second best or anything, I'd told her that if she became my stepmother and then *she* died, I'd keep a photo of her by my bed too. She'd seemed to find that quite funny.

'OK, Mum,' I told the photograph. 'Let's have a look at *your* birthday-cake recipe.'

Just before Lizzie had moved in with us, Dad had cleared a lot of our mother's stuff out of the attic and he'd given a few things to me. One thing was a big jewellery box and another was an old hairbrush from one of those fancy dressing-table sets, which I'd have liked even better if it still had some of my mother's hair in it. (When I said that to Holly she thought I was being gruesome, but I didn't think I was.) There had also been a collection of torn-out pages and magazine cuttings. One of them – which I got out now to have a closer look at – was a recipe for a kid's birthday cake, which I especially liked because it had my mother's handwriting on it. She had scrawled my brother's name – *Matty* – in blue ink in the top right-hand corner.

The cake was called *Birthday Kitten* and the picture showed two round pudding-bowl-shaped sponges, one small and one big, which had been stuck one on top of the other to make a head and body. The whole thing was covered in chocolate buttercream icing. Blue marzipan ears had been added, along with a nose, eyes and mouth and a long blue marzipan tail. Blue cocktail sticks had been used to make whiskers and the kitten had a blue ribbon round its neck. Our mother had added her own drawing at the edge of the page – a log with four candles stuck in it. She must have done that because there was no obvious place on the cake itself to put any candles. Beside her sketch she had marked the log thing with an arrow and scrawled, *choc roll???*

When I had asked Dad about it he had said that this was the cake our mother had made Matthew for his fourth birthday party. The party had taken place just a month before she had gone into hospital and died while she was giving birth to me. Dad had suggested that I give the recipe to my brother as a keepsake, but I hadn't wanted to. In the end I hadn't even shown it to Matthew, just in case he'd tried to claim it for himself. After all, he had actual memories of our mother, didn't he? So what more did he need?

But now, as I stared at my mother's photo, I wondered if Matthew ever wished she was still here with us, the way I did sometimes. I reckoned he must do. And I suddenly knew how I could make Matthew's seventeenth birthday party so special he was going to forget all about Jennifer dumping him.

'The thing about *this* birthday cake,' I told Holly when I phoned her back, 'is that it's going to be a surprise for Matty – but not just from me and you. It's also going to be a surprise from our mum!'

'*Wicked!*' Holly replied, and she offered to come round straight away so she could help make the cake when Matty went out.

'You haven't told your mum about the party, have you?' I asked anxiously. Holly's mum is a lot cooler about that sort of stuff than Dad, but I still didn't want her knowing.

'Of course not. Mum doesn't know your dad's away this weekend, and I've just told her I'm spending the night at yours. By the way, she wants to know if you fancy coming out with us for lunch today. We're going to that new Italian place in town for a pizza.'

'I will if we get the cake done in time,' I said. 'I'd better go. See you in a bit, OK?'

As soon as I got off the phone, I started to search our kitchen cupboards for cake ingredients and found that we didn't have anything except baking powder and a few eggs, so I got out my umbrella and raincoat and told my brother I was going out to buy some sweets. Instead, I went down the road to our local supermarket, where I spent a generous amount of my own money buying everything I needed for the cake. As well as the sponge ingredients, I bought marzipan, blue food colouring, cocktail sticks (though I couldn't find blue ones) and blue ribbon. I also bought a box of blue birthday candles and holders and a packet of chocolate mini rolls – I reckoned I'd need to use several if I was going to fit on seventeen candles.

I got home to find Holly already waiting for me. Unfortunately, my brother was also still there, along with Jake and another guy who looked a bit older than them. The three boys seemed to be having a practice party in our kitchen, stuffing their faces with crisps and drinking Coke straight from the two-litre bottle Dad had got in for us.

'I thought you were going out,' I said to my brother.

'We don't need to now. This is Jake's mate Keith. He already got the booze.' Matty pointed to a selection of beer and cider that was stacked on the floor. 'Listen, have you been round to feed that pest next door yet?'

I looked at Holly, who was sitting at the kitchen table (trying to hide the fact that she really liked

21

being in the same room as my brother). An idea was already forming in my head. 'We'll go and feed him now,' I said. 'Come on, Holly.'

I had left my shopping bags in the hall and, as Holly and I left the house, I picked them up to take with us. 'We can make Matthew's cake in secret in Mrs Lewis's kitchen,' I whispered. 'Matty won't notice how long we're gone now that his mates are here.'

We let ourselves in to Mrs Lewis's and the first thing I did was fill up Pixie's empty bowl. Pixie burst in through the cat flap while I was doing it, growling and clutching something between his jaws, which I instantly recognized as Hercule's favourite toy mouse – the one with the catnip in it.

'Pixie, you are so bad!' I shouted at him, snatching up the mouse as he dropped it beside his food bowl. 'He really bullies Hercule,' I complained to Holly.

'Hercule won't let him when he gets bigger,' Holly said, starting to unpack the shopping. 'Look, we'd better get a move on if we want this cake to be done by lunchtime.'

Holly and I had both baked before with her mum, so we reckoned we'd be able to follow the instructions on the cake recipe fairly easily. Fortunately, Mrs Lewis had lots of useful things in her kitchen cupboards, including two different-sized pudding basins, a big mixing bowl, weighing scales and a sieve for the flour. I still had to sneak back into my house to get our electric whisk, and I also brought back a big-enough plate to sit the finished cake on, since we didn't have a proper cake-board.

After we'd mixed up all the ingredients, we tipped the mixture into the pudding basins and put them carefully in the oven. The cakes only needed an hour to cook, so Holly and I cleared up the mess in the kitchen while we were waiting. Then, when the two sponges were done, we took them out of the oven and tipped them out on to a wire rack to cool.

That's when we heard a noise at the front door. Pixie heard it too and immediately stopped washing his paws to make a hasty exit through the cat flap. Someone was out on the porch, trying to unlock the door, and it sounded like they were having a bit of trouble with the keys.

'It must be Basil,' I gasped, remembering that Mrs Lewis's son had told Matty he'd be coming here today. For a second or two I froze. Then I quickly shut the kitchen door and wedged a chair-back under the handle. 'We can get out the back way,' I told Holly. 'I've got the key.' It was just as well I did, I thought, since there was no sign of Mrs Lewis's own back-door key anywhere.

I couldn't help wondering what Basil would do when he got inside the house, and I pressed my ear against the kitchen door for a couple of minutes to listen. I heard him move through the hall into the living room and then I heard him moving around in there, opening and closing cupboards and drawers as if he was searching for something.

'He's looking for the jewellery or whatever it is,' I whispered. 'Mrs Lewis was right. He *is* going to steal something from her!'

'Esmie, let's get out of here,' Holly hissed. 'What if he finds us?'

'He can't while the chair's like that.' Matty had used the chair-under-the-door-handle method to block his bedroom door at home sometimes to stop *me* going in, so I knew from personal experience how effective it was.

'Esmie, come *on*! You don't even know for sure that it's her son. What if it's a real burglar?'

'He had a key, didn't he? It *must* be Basil.'

We quickly let ourselves out, locking the back door again from the outside as quietly as we could.

'What if he gets into the kitchen and sees the cakes?' Holly said as we hurried down the path that led along the side of Mrs Lewis's house.

'He'll just think his mother must have baked them before she went into hospital.'

'But, Esmie, they're still *warm*.'

'Don't worry – he won't be able to get into the kitchen anyway.' A car – it had to be Basil's – was now parked in Mrs Lewis's driveway and I stopped to stare at it. 'Anyway, he won't care about the cakes,' I said. 'All *he* cares about is stealing Mrs Lewis's treasure before she gets out of hospital, and you know what?' I rapped the bonnet of his getaway car with my knuckle. 'I'm not going to let him!'

'*What?*' Holly stood gaping at me as I started walking towards Mrs Lewis's porch.

'When he answers the door, I'll say I saw him arrive and that his mother's told me *all* about him!' I called back to her in a loud whisper. 'That way I might *scare* him into stopping whatever he's doing!'

'But, Esmie, what if he's dangerous?'

I paused on the porch steps, remembering all the warnings I'd had from Dad about how you should never put yourself in a vulnerable position with strangers. Basil didn't feel like a stranger, because I knew his mother. On the other hand, if his own mother didn't trust him not to steal from her, then who knew what else he might be capable of? 'Maybe we'd better get Matty to come with us,' I said reluctantly.

Holly nodded, looking relieved. 'Come on then,' she said, leading the way back towards my house – and my brother.

Unfortunately, Matty was in a bad mood when we got in. When I told him that Mrs Lewis's son was next door, all he said was, '*So?*' And when I added that we'd actually *heard* Basil rooting around in his mother's stuff while we were in the kitchen, feeding Pixie, Matty seemed to think there was some perfectly innocent explanation. 'He's probably just collecting up some of her clothes and things to take to the hospital,' he said. 'What did he say he was doing when you asked him?'

'We didn't ask him. We sneaked out of the house while he was still in the front room.'

'*What*? You mean you were in the kitchen and you didn't even call out to tell him you were there?'

'No – we wanted to see what he'd do.'

'Esmie, you'd better not get into any trouble while Dad's away, because I'm meant to be looking after you and *I'm* the one who's going to get the blame for it!' That's when I found out that Dad had phoned while I'd been gone, and that he hadn't been too impressed when Matty had gone off to fetch me and come back rather sheepishly to say that he couldn't find me anywhere in the house.

'Why didn't you just tell him I'd gone next door to feed Pixie?' I asked. 'You knew that's where we were.'

'You went next door ages ago. I assumed you'd be back by now. What the hell have you been doing over there all this time anyway?'

'Well . . .' I quickly tried to think up a suitable excuse for why we'd been gone so long – and I couldn't. 'So where did you tell Dad I was then?' I asked instead.

Matty scowled like that was a sore point. 'I made out like I'd *just remembered* you'd gone next door and then he started going on about how if the house caught fire, he hoped I wouldn't *just remember* afterwards that you were still in it!'

I pulled a sympathetic face. 'Sounds like he's in a bad mood.'

'Too right he is! Apparently their cottage is grotty and it's rained ever since they got there – so of course he's taking it out on me.' He went back into the living room, slamming the door behind him.

Holly and I went upstairs to my bedroom to have a bit of a powwow, and when the doorbell rang about ten minutes later we let Matty answer it.

'It's probably another one of his mates,' I grunted. 'Or *Jake's* mates . . .' Jake himself was OK, but I didn't like some of the older boys he hung out with, and I was a bit worried that Matty's party tonight might get pretty wild if Jake had too much to do with the guest list.

Holly and I were just debating whether or not we should phone Dad on his mobile to tell *him* about Basil stealing Mrs Lewis's treasure (because he is a policeman, after all), when Matthew called upstairs to me, '*Esmie!* Have we got the key to Mrs Lewis's back door? Her son's here and he needs to get into her kitchen.'

❋ 5 ❋

'Holly, you go down and stall them!' I hissed.

When I eventually got downstairs, clutching Mrs Lewis's key ring, from which I had just removed the back door key, Holly was standing awkwardly in the hall, gawping at our visitor as if he was an alien.

'Esmie, this is Mrs Lewis's son,' Matty told me. 'The kitchen door in his mother's house has got jammed or something.'

'Are you *Basil*?' I asked, looking straight at the man, who was actually quite ordinary-looking – tall and thin with grey hair and a perfectly unremarkable face. But probably the most successful criminals were the ones who could slip into the background like that. 'Mrs Lewis has told me about you,' I added, trying to make my voice sound ominous but clearly failing, since Basil immediately looked flattered.

'Has she really?' he said. 'She must be getting sentimental in her old age.' He had a disappointingly ordinary voice too.

I quickly told him that we didn't have the back-door key to Mrs Lewis's house – only the front one.

'I don't understand how the kitchen door can be jammed,' Matty said. 'Esmie's only just been in there to feed Pixie.'

'It was all right then, wasn't it, Holly?' I lied, avoiding looking at anyone except her.

My friend avoided looking at anyone too as she nodded.

'Do you want me to come over and try to help you open it?' my brother asked, but Basil glanced through into the living room, where Jake and Keith were laughing at something on the television, and said, 'No, no, it's OK. I've got to get home now, but I'll bring some tools with me when I come back this evening.'

'You're coming back this evening?' I gasped before I could stop myself.

'I'll have to get into her kitchen somehow,' Basil replied. 'Thanks for feeding her cat, by the way.' He suddenly frowned. 'You know, I bet that wretched animal's knocked something on to the floor and it's jammed under the door. He's always causing one problem or another. He certainly wasn't in the rest of the house. I checked before I came out.'

After Basil had gone, my brother immediately launched into accusing Holly and me of somehow accidentally damaging the door ourselves when we'd left. Holly started to say that we had used the back door to leave by, but I stopped her. If Matty knew we'd used the back door then he'd know I must have been lying about not having the key.

'I wonder why Basil's so desperate to get into the kitchen,' I said to Holly as we went back up to my room. 'Do you think it's because he hasn't found what he's looking for yet, and he thinks it might be there?'

'Well . . .' Holly looked thoughtful. 'My grandma keeps her diamond ring in a plastic bag at the bottom of a sugar container in *her* kitchen, because she says no burglar would ever think of looking there. Mrs Lewis might have hidden this jewellery, or whatever it is, somewhere like that.'

'Let's go and look right now!' I said, getting excited, but that's when Holly reminded me that her mum was collecting us in a few minutes, to take us out to lunch.

'We'd better go straight out to the car as soon as she pulls up. If she comes to the door she'll expect your dad to be here.'

So I went out for a pizza with Holly and her mum, and afterwards we went back to Holly's to collect her overnight stuff before her mum dropped us both off at mine again. Thankfully, it was still pouring with rain, so Holly's mum didn't want to get out of the car and come in to have a chat with Dad and Lizzie like she normally does.

It was almost half past three by the time Holly

and I let ourselves into Mrs Lewis's house again through the back door. We found Pixie curled up on a chair, but he jumped down as soon as he saw us and immediately started yowling to be fed. He was a very greedy cat as well as a bad-tempered one, I decided. Thankfully though, he hadn't disturbed the cakes we had left on the side, and as I opened a tin of cat food for him, Holly started to search in Mrs Lewis's sugar tin. Finding nothing there except sugar, she turned to the tea-caddy, which she reckoned might also be a good hiding place for a precious heirloom that you didn't actually want your heir to get his hands on. I quickly joined in the search and we must have spent half an hour scouring the kitchen after that, but to no avail.

'Well,' I concluded when we'd finished, 'at least if *we* can't find it, then Basil won't be able to either. We'd better just get on with making Matty's cake.'

We made the chocolate buttercream and spread it over both cakes, then placed the smaller sponge on top of the larger one to make a head and body before using a lot more buttercream to get them to stick together, like it said in the recipe. Then we got to the fun part. By the time we'd finished, we had blue food colouring all over our hands, but we'd also made a really cute face for our kitten and a long blue marzipan tail. The wooden cocktail sticks looked fine as whiskers and we'd also used a couple to fix on the marzipan ears. Lastly I opened the packet of chocolate mini rolls and used three of them to stick all the candles in.

When we'd cleared up the kitchen, Holly looked at her watch and said, 'We'd better get out of here. I'll hold the umbrella up if you carry the cake.'

As she spoke, there was an impatient ringing on the front doorbell and we heard my brother's voice yelling at us through the letter box. 'Esmie, are you in there?'

I quickly removed the chair that we'd left blocking the kitchen door just in case Basil should return earlier than expected, and went out into the hall. 'We're just feeding Pixie!' I called out to him. 'I'll be home in a minute!'

'Esmie, let me in – NOW!'

'He mustn't see the cake!' Holly hissed, joining me in the hall and closing the kitchen door firmly behind her.

We opened the front door and saw that my brother was very worked up about something. He had on his long black winter coat, but he didn't have an umbrella and his hair was wet. He didn't even ask what we were doing or how we'd managed to get into the kitchen – he was too flustered. 'Esmie, you've got to come and speak to Dad. He's on the phone and he's livid! I told him you were in your room, and then I went to fetch you and you weren't there, so I told him you were probably feeding

Pixie, but he's insisting on speaking to you right now!'

'I don't understand why he's panicking so much,' I answered crossly. 'He's treating me like I'm a baby or something.'

'Tell me about it!' Matthew grunted. 'I said to him, "Look, Dad, do you really think I've lost her and I'm too scared to tell you or something?" and he blew up at me for giving him lip. He's really gone off on one and it's all your fault! Why do you have to keep disappearing every five minutes?'

I nearly retorted that the reason I kept disappearing was that I was *trying* to do something nice for *him* – but I stopped myself. The birthday cake was already made, and I didn't want anything to spoil the surprise now.

❀ 6 ❀

It was still raining heavily when Holly and I went back to collect the cake later on, while Matty was out buying last-minute stuff for the party. There was no sign of Basil. Pixie was curled up on a kitchen chair again and, judging from the muddy paw prints everywhere, he had been conducting his own exploration of the kitchen while we'd been gone. The paw prints on the kitchen table formed a ring around the cake, but we couldn't see any obvious lick marks on the buttercream.

'He probably doesn't like chocolate,' I pointed out.

'Maybe not,' Holly replied, but I could see she was planning to scrape off any icing she got on *her* slice of cake, just the same.

We carried the cake back home underneath Dad's big umbrella and took it up to my bedroom, where I placed it carefully on the table I use to do my homework. Then I turned my mother's photograph round so she could look at it. I could tell Holly thought I was daft to do that, but she didn't say anything. She knows what I'm like about my mother.

We started to get excited as the time for the party got nearer. We put on make-up and made our hair look really funky and got changed into our most grown-up clothes, while Matty had a shower and gelled his hair and put on his favourite shirt and a clean pair of jeans. I took it as a good sign that he cared how he looked even though Jennifer had dumped him.

Pretty soon lots of people started to arrive. Most of them were in Matty's year at school and some of them were teenagers we knew, or at least had spoken to once or twice because they lived nearby, but there were also some complete strangers who didn't even seem to know Jake very well, let alone Matty.

'We'll bring the cake downstairs once the party gets going properly,' I told Holly.

An hour later, the music was on full blast and I was just opening the front door to let in yet another party guest, when I saw a car pull into Mrs Lewis's drive. It was Basil! I called out to Holly, who was sitting on the stairs munching crisps, watching a girl and boy slow dancing in the hall to a track that wasn't the least bit slow.

'Basil's back!' I grabbed my coat and felt in the pocket to check that Mrs Lewis's door keys were still there. 'Let's go and see what he's doing!'

'That boy who's dancing in the hall was snogging a different girl half an hour ago,' Holly told me as she followed me down our driveway. 'Matty's not snogging anyone tonight though, is he?'

I looked at her. 'Holly, I keep telling you. There's no point in *you* fancying my brother. He's four years older than you!'

'Three years and eight months,' she corrected me.

It had stopped raining, but it still felt really damp and cold outside as we hurried across to Mrs Lewis's front porch. The music from our house sounded pretty loud even from there, and I started to worry that we'd have the neighbours complaining if we weren't careful.

'I'd better get Matty to turn the music down a bit when we get back,' I said. My brother, after the first couple of beers he'd drunk with Jake at the start of the evening, was now drinking quite a lot of Coke rather than anything else. In fact, I got the feeling he was trying, at least for now, to keep a bit of control over both himself and the party. He'd asked me twice if I was OK, and I'd come out of the bathroom a little while ago to find him telling some couple, who were about to go into my bedroom, that the upstairs rooms were out of bounds. He'd gone to check Dad and Lizzie's room after that, but thankfully nobody was in there.

I peered into Mrs Lewis's house through the letter box, trying to see inside.

'Can you see him?' Holly asked, crouching down behind me.

'No. Let's go round the back and look in through the kitchen window.'

We hurried round the side of the house and found that the light was on in the kitchen and the blind was open. Basil was rummaging around in his mother's kitchen drawers, just like we had done ourselves earlier that day. Suddenly he went out into the hall again but we could still see him from the window. He was opening a drawer in the hall table. As we watched, he slid it right out and brought it back into the kitchen with him, setting it down on the table there and starting to take things out of it. He removed what looked like an address book and then some bundles of papers and some envelopes, including a large brown one. He tipped the envelope up and shook its contents on to the table, and from the way his face lit up we knew he'd finally found what he'd been looking for. But we still couldn't see what it was because the drawer itself was obscuring our view.

Basil was clearly delighted though. He started to put the other things back in the drawer, ready to make his getaway.

I'm not a police detective's daughter for nothing. 'We've got to stop him!' I blurted out. I raced back round to the front of the house, with Holly close behind me, and used Mrs Lewis's front-door key to lock the door from the outside. I told Holly to hold our key in the keyhole so that Basil wouldn't be able to get his own key into the lock and would therefore be trapped inside. 'Stay here and make sure he doesn't escape while I go and phone Dad and ask him what to do,' I instructed her.

'I'm not staying here on my own!' Holly protested. 'Why don't *you* stay here and *I'll* phone your dad?'

So I told Holly where to find Dad's mobile number and that when she rang him, she should make it clear that this was an emergency. 'Ask him if we should phone 999?'

But before Holly had even set off towards our house, another car I recognized turned into the street.

Holly looked at me and gasped, 'Isn't that . . . ?'

I nodded, feeling my own mouth drop open. As if by magic, Dad had arrived home just when we needed him most!

Basil had come to the front door now and was trying to open it from inside.

'Over here, Dad! *Quickly!*' I yelled, as my father and Lizzie stepped out of the car and Holly shot off to warn Matthew they were back.

As Dad came over to join me on Mrs Lewis's porch, the music from our own house had clearly caught his attention. 'Esmie, what's going on over there?' he demanded. 'And why are you wearing all that make-up?'

'Dad, thank goodness you're here!' I burst out, ignoring his questions. I could see Lizzie following Holly into our house, but I didn't have time to worry about that now. 'Mrs Lewis's son is trying to steal something from her! She warned me about him and now he's inside and we've got to stop him.' At that moment, Basil started to shout angrily from the other side of the door, demanding to be let out.

Everything happened really quickly then. Dad moved me out of the way and unlocked the door, Basil emerged, looking furious, and the music from our house stopped abruptly.

I explained everything to Dad as Basil stood in his mother's hallway, gaping at me in astonishment. He was keeping a tight grip on the brown envelope, I noticed.

When Basil heard what his mother had said to me, he put on a very puzzled look. 'But what treasure could she think I wanted to steal from her?'

'That,' I said, pointing at the envelope. 'You just took it from the drawer in the hall. Holly and I saw you through the kitchen window.'

'Esmie—' Dad began, but Basil interrupted him.

'Listen,' he said impatiently, 'what I've been looking for is my mother's passport. The two of us haven't been that close in recent years, but I want to try and patch things up by taking her on a surprise holiday when she gets out of hospital. I'm hoping she'll agree to put Pixie in a cattery for a bit if it means she gets to come with me to America. My son lives there with my ex-wife. He's her only grand-child and I think he's probably the only person in the world she actually rates higher than that damn cat! The thing is, she's coming home tomorrow – she's only sprained her ankle rather than broken it, thank goodness – and I want to get this holiday sorted out before she gets back. That's why I need her passport.' As if Basil thought I might need fur-ther proof, he opened the envelope to show me.

'Oops,' I muttered, when I saw that he was clearly speaking the truth – about the contents of the envelope at least.

'*Oops*?' Dad was looking at me crossly now. 'Is that all you've got to say for yourself, miss?'

'Sorry,' I mumbled, and as Dad apologized to Basil and placed his hands firmly on my shoulders to march me home, I knew I was in big trouble – in fact, Basil actually looked like he felt sorry for me.

I couldn't believe I'd got it so wrong – and I still didn't understand what Mrs Lewis had meant when she'd warned me about Basil – but I had other things to worry about now.

'The party was Matty's idea,' I told Dad quickly as we approached the house and a group of laugh-ing teenagers emerged from it, some of them still swigging cans of beer. Lots more people were making their exit via the back door, coming out down the side path on to the driveway.

Lizzie and Holly came out of the front door, behind Keith and two older boys. Holly was clutching her overnight bag and pulling a sympathetic face at me as she quickly dodged past Dad.

'John, I think I'd better take Holly home,' Lizzie said. 'I've told Matthew he has to get everyone to leave.'

Lizzie wasn't daft, I thought, as I watched her get into her car and escape from our house with my friend.

'Right,' Dad said in a gruff voice as he pushed me inside, 'let's go and find your brother, shall we?'

Matty was in the living room, hastily shoving empty beer cans and cider bottles into a black plastic bag. When Dad and I appeared in the doorway, he looked like he was going to be sick. 'Dad,' he gasped hoarsely.

'Matthew,' Dad replied grimly.

Matty swallowed. 'Just a few friends round . . .'

'A *few* friends?' Dad was looking round the room. It was empty of people now, but there were pizza boxes on the coffee table, beer cans and empty bottles everywhere, crisps trodden into the carpet and a triangle of pepperoni pizza wedged down the side of the sofa. Dad and Lizzie's CDs, as well as Matty's, had all been tipped out in a big pile over by the stereo. Some people had been smoking – you could still smell it – and an ornamental mug (that was practically an antique because it had belonged to Dad's father) had been taken down off the mantelpiece and used as an ashtray.

Dad picked up the mug and looked at my brother.

Matty instantly went red. 'Sorry, Dad – I didn't see that.'

'What? Or you'd have cleared it up with the rest of the evidence?' Dad was pointing at the black bag with the beer cans in it.

'Some of the people were eighteen so it was legal for them to drink,' I told Dad quickly.

But Dad ignored me. He looked incapable of further speech because he had just spotted the piece of pepperoni pizza. As Matty hurriedly retrieved it, Dad put one hand on his shoulder and pointed him in the direction of the door. 'Let's take a tour of the rest of the house, shall we?' He pushed my brother in front of him through the hall – which was thankfully empty – into the kitchen, which was full of party debris too. The drinks cupboard had been opened, and all Dad's liqueurs and the cheap sherry Lizzie had bought at Christmas to put in the trifle were out on the side with their lids off. The back door had been left open so it was totally freezing, and when Dad went over to shut it he found a couple of teenagers still snogging out in the garden.

I thought that upstairs would be OK. But when Dad looked in his own bedroom, the drawers and wardrobe had been opened and some of Lizzie's underwear had been draped across the bed along with an especially sexy nightie that Dad had bought for her.

Matty went even redder.

'Matthew told them no one was allowed upstairs, didn't you, Matty?' I said, trying to help, but Dad was already snatching up Lizzie's clothes and throwing them in a more decent pile on top of the bedroom chair. As he did that, he suddenly noticed the dressing table, where a beer bottle had been plonked down. He lifted it up, exposing a wet ring on the polished surface.

Matty was slowly backing out of the room, looking like he knew that at any minute now he was really going to get it. He stumbled across the landing to his own room, started to go inside, then seemed to dart out again just as quickly, heading for my bedroom instead.

As Dad and I followed, I did my best to stall our father. 'Dad, why are you back so early anyhow?' I asked.

'Because the weather was lousy, the cottage was damp and those damn walking boots were giving me blisters,' Dad snapped. 'And because I had a feeling your brother couldn't be trusted!'

Matty quickly closed the door of my bedroom behind him.

It crossed my mind that Matty might put a chair under the door handle to block it, but at the same time I knew he wouldn't dare do that to Dad – not if he wanted to actually survive this evening. Dad crossed the landing and flung open my door. As I followed him inside, I nearly crashed straight into the back of him.

Inside my room, Dad and Matthew were standing absolutely still, both staring at the same thing. In all the excitement I had completely forgotten about my birthday surprise for Matty.

'I made it from that recipe, Dad!' I said quickly. 'The one we found in the loft.'

Dad didn't even look at me. He just kept staring at the cake. His face had totally changed. Instead of looking angry, he looked . . . well . . . as if he was remembering something from a long time ago.

Matthew, however, didn't seem to recognize the cake at all. 'What *is* it?' he asked.

'It's a birthday cake of course. It's meant to be for *you*! Holly and I baked it, but it's not just from us . . .' When he didn't seem to get what I meant, I picked up the recipe with our mother's handwriting on and handed it to him. 'Don't you remember it at all?' I couldn't believe I had gone to all this trouble and Matty had no memory of our mother's original birthday surprise.

As Matty looked at the recipe, he said, 'I don't know what you're talking about, Esmie.' He glanced at Dad.

Dad clearly *did* remember the original cake, and he was looking at this one as if he was seeing not a sticky iced sponge in the shape of a cat, but my mother herself – and a much younger Matthew.

Slowly he turned to look at my brother. 'Mummy made you that cake for your fourth birthday,' he told him.

My brother looked stunned. 'Huh?'

'Esmie's used your mother's recipe to make you the same cake,' Dad explained quietly, looking at me. 'Right, Esmie?' As I nodded, he turned back to Matthew. 'Don't you remember it? A lot else happened soon after that, of course – perhaps you don't . . .' He broke off, sitting down heavily on my bed.

My brother stayed standing, shifting his gaze from the cake, to Dad, to me, then back to the cake again. But he was slowly relaxing a bit now that Dad had calmed down. Our father can get absolutely furious, especially with Matthew, but when it's over, it's over. Dad hardly ever gets a second wind. Matty's gaze eventually settled on me. 'Ez, you are really something, you know that?' he murmured.

'It was Holly's idea to make you a birthday cake to cheer you up,' I said. 'But it was my idea to use our mum's recipe – to make it a surprise from her too, if you know what I mean . . .' I broke off, feeling a bit self-conscious.

But Matthew was looking at me as if he understood – and he actually looked grateful.

'Why would your brother need cheering up?' Dad suddenly asked.

I looked at Matty to see if he was going to tell him.

My brother sighed. Then he plonked himself wearily down on the bed beside Dad. 'Jennifer dumped me,' he grunted.

Dad didn't look totally surprised – I'm not sure he ever thought that Matty and Jennifer were that well suited – but he did look sympathetic. 'So when did this happen?'

'Just after you left yesterday. She rang me to tell me. I guess she thought it was easier to chuck me over the phone.' Matty spoke in a trying-to-sound-cool voice, but when Dad put his arm round him, Matty leaned his head against Dad's shoulder in a way that wasn't so cool at all.

A few minutes later we heard Lizzie coming in, and Matthew quickly pulled away from Dad and stood up.

'I think you two had better get to bed now,' Dad said, standing up himself. 'We'll talk about this in the morning, Matthew – along with a few other things.' Dad was starting to sound quite firm again and I knew that tomorrow Matty was going to be spending the day cleaning up our house, relinquishing his allowance to pay for anything that was damaged, and getting intermittently lectured by Dad about how irresponsible he'd been and how, if he couldn't act like a grown-up, then he wasn't going to get treated like one. I wasn't sure how much I was going to be roped into the clearing up – but I reckoned Dad was going to make me do my bit since I'd clearly colluded with my brother, even if the party hadn't been my actual idea.

'Umm . . . Dad . . . the trouble is . . .' my brother muttered. 'My bedroom's already . . . er . . . occupied . . .'

'*What?*'

'I just looked in there and Jake's asleep on the bed. He was meant to be checking nobody was in the bedrooms. I guess he must have conked out.'

We all went though to Matty's room to find Jake lying on top of my brother's bed, fully clothed and fast asleep. Dad, who's known Jake since he was little, stood looking at him for a moment, then went over and pulled off his boots. 'Do his parents know he's here?'

'Well, yeah . . .' Matty mumbled. 'He told them he'd be staying over.'

'Right, well you can take the floor then, can't you?'

And as my brother followed Dad though to the cupboard where we keep the spare bedding, I thought that Dad definitely hadn't forgiven Matthew yet for throwing this party – and probably wouldn't for quite a while.

The following morning while Matty and I were cleaning up the living room – Jake had escaped home before Dad could recruit him as well – the doorbell rang. Dad, who was with Lizzie in the kitchen preparing a roast lunch for us all, went to answer it.

'Esmie!' he called out after a moment or two, and I went to the door to find Mrs Lewis and her son standing on our porch. Mrs Lewis's leg was bandaged up and she was using a stick to lean on, but she looked pretty healthy apart from that.

'I've just been to collect my mother from the hospital,' Basil said, 'and before I took her inside she insisted on coming to thank you for looking after Pixie.'

'That's right,' Mrs Lewis said, actually smiling at me – which she'd never done before. 'You're a very good girl, to look after my darling boy while I was away.' Behind her I could see Basil pulling a face. Clearly he didn't think that Pixie was a darling boy at all.

As she spoke, Pixie himself leaped over the low fence between our two driveways and bounded up to join us on the porch. He flung himself against Mrs Lewis's bad leg and started to rub himself ferociously against it.

'Careful—' Basil began, looking worried, but Mrs Lewis's face had lit up as Pixie appeared.

'How are you, my treasure?' she crooned, bending down to stroke him.

I gaped at her. 'Your *treasure*?'

'Oh yes! You're Mummy's treasure, aren't you, pusskins?'

Basil was giving me a pointed look now.

'Were you worried in case Basil got rid of *Pixie* while you were away?' I asked incredulously.

Mrs Lewis scowled at her son. 'Well, I wouldn't put it past him!'

'You know I wouldn't find a new home for Pixie without asking you, Mother!' Basil protested. 'Though, like I keep saying, I do worry that he's getting too much for you and—'

'Nonsense!' Mrs Lewis interrupted fiercely. 'My Pixie and I belong together.'

As Basil led his mother across to her own house, I looked up at Dad. 'So *that* was what she meant when she said to make sure Basil didn't get his hands on her treasure!'

Dad was shaking his head, looking half amused

and half exasperated. 'I really wish you'd think more before you act sometimes, Esmie.'

'I *do* think before I act!' I protested. 'I *thought* Basil was trying to steal some really precious jewellery from her or something. I mean, how was I to know he was only searching for her passport?' As Dad closed our front door, I added, 'I wonder if she'll agree to go away on holiday with him. It doesn't sound like he's told her yet, does it?'

'Well, he did say he wanted it to be a surprise,' Dad pointed out.

'Talking of surprises . . .' Lizzie said, coming out of the kitchen to join us, 'what a wonderful idea, Esmie – to make Matthew that birthday cake! But how on earth did you do it without Matty seeing you?'

'Well –' I decided it was best not to mention the fact that I'd borrowed Mrs Lewis's kitchen – and half her baking equipment – without asking – 'It *was* tricky . . . but it helped that Matty was pretty distracted.'

'I bet he was,' Dad snorted.

'I meant because of Jennifer,' I said, 'not the party.'

Matthew had come into the hall as he heard his name, and now Lizzie put her hand on his shoulder affectionately. 'I asked your dad how long it took *him* to clean up the house after the party *he* threw when he was your age,' she told him. 'He says it took the whole of the next day – so I think you're doing pretty well.'

Matthew and I both stared at Dad. '*You* threw a party?'

'Teenage boys are all the same, I reckon,' Dad replied, looking slightly amused by our reaction. 'Not that *my* guests were anywhere near as badly behaved as yours, Matthew. Our house was almost as good as new by the time *my* parents got home – which was just as well, because my father wasn't as mild-tempered as I am.'

'Yeah . . . right . . .' Matty grunted.

Lizzie laughed, and even Dad smiled, which he doesn't normally do when Matthew is cheeky to him.

'So when are we going to cut Matthew's birthday cake?' I asked eagerly. 'His birthday's not for another month and it might not keep very well until then.'

'Well . . .' Dad turned to Lizzie. 'Lunch is in the oven, but it'll be a couple of hours before it's ready.'

Lizzie nodded. 'Would you like us to do it now, Esmie?'

'Hey, it's *my* birthday cake!' Matty pointed out indignantly, but he quickly shut up as he got a look from Dad that was probably a lot like the one he'd got when he was four and had threatened to throw a tantrum in the middle of pass the parcel.

So we all went into the kitchen and Dad took our

biggest knife out of the cutlery drawer and presented it to my brother.

'We've got to light the candles first,' I said. 'Then Matty can get to blow them out and make a wish.'

'Esmie, I'm not into all that kids' stuff any more,' Matty protested, but I had already picked up the matches.

Dad and Matthew and I were all standing close together beside the cake, and even Hercule had come into the kitchen and was rubbing his head against my ankle as if he knew that this was an important family occasion. Only Lizzie stood a little further back. Dad quickly reached for her hand and drew her nearer.

'If you don't want your wish, then *I'll* have it,' I told my brother when all seventeen candles were lit.

'Be my guest,' he said.

So Matty and I blew out the candles while Lizzie and Dad stood holding hands, watching us.

And I *did* make a wish – one that would be good for all four of us – but I can't tell you what it was. If I did, it might not come true!

Our lucky winner and her mum will each

win a **LUXURY PAMPERING**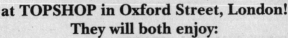

SHOPPING SPREE

at **TOPSHOP** in Oxford Street, London!

They will both enjoy:

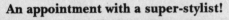

- An appointment with a super-stylist!
- Access to luxury VIP fitting rooms
- Lunch at the mouth-watering TOPSHOP kitchen
- A Nails Inc. manicure
- £150 each spending money in TOPSHOP!
- One night's accommodation in a top London hotel

To enter, log on to **www.gwynethrees.com** or fill in this page (front and back), cut it out and send to:

World Book Day Shopping Spree Competition, Marketing Department, Macmillan Children's Books, 20 New Wharf Road, London N1 9RR

Simply tell us in no more than fifty words why your mum is **THE BEST MUM IN THE UNIVERSE!**

(Attach a separate piece of paper if necessary, then turn over to fill in your details!)

_____

_____

_____

_____

_____

_____

_____

For more magical comps, dreamy downloads AND to join Gwyneth's VIP club, check out www.gwynethrees.com

Visit soon for the winning entry and photos from the day itself!

My name: _____

My age: _____

My parent/guardian's signature:

_____

(You must get your parent/guardian's signature
if you are under twelve years old)

My telephone no: _____

My address: _____

_____

_____ **Postcode:** _____